Today I Feel Like A Warm Fuzzy

Today I Feel Like A Warm Fuzzy

William L. Coleman

BETHANY HOUSE PUBLISHERS
Minneapolis, Minnesota 55438
A Division of Bethany Fellowship, Inc.

Scripture verses marked TLB are taken from The Living Bible, copyright 1971 by Tyndale House Publishers, Wheaton, Ill. Used by permission.

Photos by: Cliff Dahlen, Jon Dugan, Dick Easterday, Fred Renich, Larry Swenson and John Thornberg.

Published by Bethany House Publishers
A Division of Bethany Fellowship, Inc.
6820 Auto Club Road, Minneapolis, Minnesota 55438

Printed in the United States of America

Library of Congress Cataloging in Publication Data

Coleman, William L.
  Today I feel like a warm fuzzy.

  SUMMARY: A collection of devotions with related Bible verses that help young Christians identify and respond to their feelings.
  1. Children—Prayer-books and devotions—English.
[1. Prayer books and devotions]   I. Title.
BV4870.C637   242'.62   80-19708
ISBN 0-87123-565-X

Dedicated to

June Coleman

Acknowledgment

A special thanks to Mary Coleman for typing and preparing the manuscript.

WILLIAM L. COLEMAN is the well-known author of nearly three dozen books on a wide variety of topics. Combining his vast experience as a pastor, researcher, writer and speaker, Bill is noted for his effective devotional writing in the area of family relationships. He has been married for over twenty years and is the father of three children.

Other Books in the Coleman Family Devotional Series

Animals That Show and Tell
Listen to the Animals
If Animals Could Talk
Singing Penguins and Puffed-Up Toads
Before You Tuck Me In
Counting Stars
Good Night Book
Sleep Tight Book
My Magnificent Machine
More About My Magnificent Machine
On Your Mark
Today I Feel Like a Warm Fuzzy
Today I Feel Loved
Today I Feel Shy
Warm Hug Book

Other Books on Special Family Topics by Coleman

Getting Ready for Our New Baby
Making TV Work for Your Family
Getting Ready for My First Day of School
My Hospital Book

Contents

Feeling Good

It's important to feel good about ourselves. When we have a healthy attitude, we're free to help others.

The Bible talks about feelings. When we sit down and discuss them, our children benefit tremendously.

May your children grow to understand their feelings and how normal those feelings are. As they learn, they can better sort out the good ones from the harmful. In the process, God will do His great work in His children.

William L. Coleman
Aurora, Nebraska

Today I Feel Afraid

The little girl wanted
To climb into her mother's bed.
She had watched a television show,
And now she felt afraid.

Her mother let her in,
And the girl went right to sleep.
The next morning she had
Forgotten all about the show.

It's easy to become afraid.
There are so many things
We don't understand.
There are lots of things
We can't see.
There are many noises
We can't explain.

My old black dog
Used to climb the stairs
Late at night.
At first I didn't know
What the noise was.
Then I remembered
It was old Blackie.
And my fear went away.

Some things might make you afraid
But you've told no one about it.
They are secrets
You keep inside.

If you could explain your fear
To someone,
You might feel better.

Maybe your parents or teacher
Could explain it to you.
Then you wouldn't have to be
Afraid.

All of us are afraid at times.
It makes us feel better
To talk about it
With someone close.

"But when I am afraid, I will put my confidence in you. Yea, I will trust the promises of God."(Ps. 56:13, TLB)

Today I Feel Big

You are big!
You aren't as big
As your parents,
Or as big
As a building,
Or as big
As a truck.
But you are big!

You are bigger
Than a kitten.
You are bigger
Than an ant.
You are bigger
Than a ball.
You are bigger
Than a watermelon.

You are much bigger
Than a baby.

You are big!

If you really
Want to know
How big you are,
Raise your arms
Straight up in the air.
How big are you
From your feet
To the top of your fingers?
That's big!

When you are big
You want to be kind
To people and animals
That are smaller than you.

Big people can help
Little kittens
And feed them.

Big people can help
Smaller children
And treat them nicely.
Big people don't need
To talk loudly
Or push younger children
Or take things.

Big people, like you,
Can help little children,
And be kind.

"And if . . . you give even a cup of cold water to a little child, you will surely be rewarded."(Matt. 10:42, TLB)

Today I Feel Like Being Alone

Jeanne sometimes
Likes to be alone.
She will pick up her dolls,
Take a coloring book,
And go to her room.

When Jeanne feels this way,
She doesn't want a television set.
She even hopes her friends will stay away.
She certainly doesn't want her brother around.

Jeanne needs to be alone once in a while.
It makes her feel good.
She can think,
She can dream,
She can pretend,
She can look at things
All by herself.

Jeanne likes to talk,
But she doesn't want to talk all the time.
Jeanne likes to be read to,
But not all the time.

There is something happy
About being alone.
You can hum to yourself.
You can draw pictures for yourself.
You can talk to God
All alone.

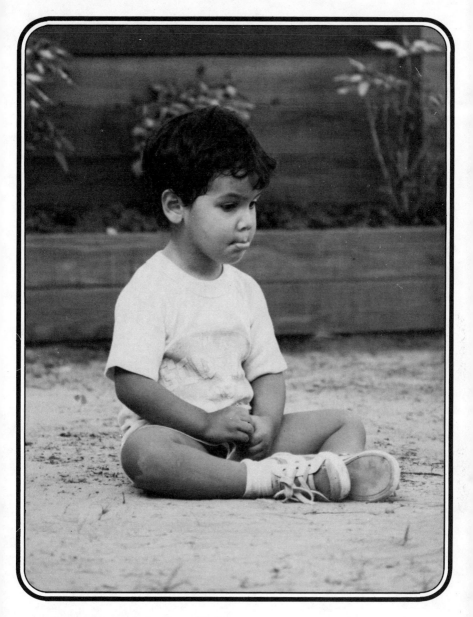

It is a peaceful, quiet feeling.
Jeanne really enjoys that—
Once in a while.

**"Yet I will not be alone,
For the Father is with me."**(John 16:32, TLB)

Today I Feel Funny

My children like to hide
In the closet.
When I open the door
To hang up my coat,
They surprise me.

We all enjoy it
Because it's fun,
And we like to laugh together.

That is why we play games
And wrestle on the floor.

Some things in life are very serious—
But not everything.
God also wants us
To have fun together.

God doesn't want us to hurt anyone
Or make them feel bad by what we say.
But God is happy to see a large smile
On our face and a laugh in our voice.

When children have fun
That isn't silly.
When their parents tell them
To be quiet,
Children can do that, too.

When you feel like being funny
And the time is right,
Really enjoy yourself.
God likes to hear you laugh.

"A time to laugh."(Eccles. 3:4, TLB)

Today I Feel Angry

It happens to everyone.
We all get angry.
So angry, sometimes,
We want to hit, scream,
Or break something.

Sometimes it's all right to get angry.
If you see your friend
Stealing candy from a store,

Or if a bully is picking on someone
Smaller than him,
You should be upset.

The Bible says Jesus became angry
When people misused God's house.

But sometimes anger is selfish.
"I want my own way"
Is an attitude that causes
This kind of sinful anger.
Jesus can help you to choose
The right feelings.

If you do allow yourself to get angry,
Don't hurt anyone
Or break anything.
That doesn't help.
Often it makes things worse.

If you get angry
Because something is really bad,
Don't stay angry for long.
If you forget about it,
You will be happy much sooner.

If we stay angry for days,
We will be miserable.
The sooner we drop our anger
The more quickly we can be happy again.

If you are still angry,
Ask Jesus to take it away.
God will help you choose
To be happy again.

"If you are angry, don't sin by nursing your grudge. Don't let the sun go down with you still angry — get over it quickly."(Eph. 4:26, TLB)

Today I Feel Gentle

Rob likes to play ball.
When he runs with the ball,
His legs pump hard
And he moves fast.

Rob also likes to build things.
He hits the nails as hard as he can.
The hammer makes a loud noise.

He is strong and active
And he likes to do things.

But Rob also likes to do
Gentle things.

Rob enjoys books
And he likes to color
And he listens to music.
In the evening
Rob plays quietly
With his cars.

Rob can play hard.
But he can also be gentle.

Do you like
To be gentle, sometimes?

"The gentleness of Christ."(2 Cor. 10:1, KJV)

Today I Feel Like Cheating

It's easy to cheat.
When you play a game,
You might move the ball
When no one is looking.

Or, you could say you were safe
When you knew you weren't.

Cheating isn't hard,
And sometimes
No one finds out.
But cheating is wrong,
And you don't want to do
What is wrong.

It's more fun
To be honest,
To play fair,
And to tell the truth.

Being honest
Makes you feel good,
Keeps your friends happy,
And makes God glad.

"The Lord hates cheating and delights in honesty."(Prov. 11:1, TLB)

Today I Feel Like Giving

Randy is like most boys!
He enjoys getting things.
Randy likes candy, cards,
Money, balls and plastic horses.

Randy likes to keep everything.
He puts things in boxes and bags,

And pushes things into his dresser drawers,
And stuffs some things under his mattress.

Randy likes to get things
And he likes to keep them.

One day a little boy came
To visit Randy.
So Randy got some toys out
And let the little boy
Play with them.

But Randy watched his toys carefully.
He didn't want any of them
Lost or broken.

Then, suddenly, Randy got an idea.
He handed his small, red car
To his little friend.

"Here," said Randy,
"You can take this car
And you can keep it.
I have lots more."

The little boy looked up
With the brightest smile
Randy had ever seen.
"Thank you," said the boy.

Randy liked that.
He enjoyed seeing that big smile.
Giving made Randy feel good.

Since then, once in a while,
Randy gives something away.
Giving makes Randy feel happy.

"God loveth a cheerful giver."(2 Cor. 9:7, KJV)

Today I Feel Like Complaining

Have you ever seen
A person who complained
All day long?

He didn't like his breakfast.

He didn't want to wear
That pair of shoes,
Or that pair of pants.

He didn't want
To stay in the house,
But he didn't want to go out.

Everything was wrong
And no one could make him happy.

When a person complains
All day long,
He isn't much fun
To be around.

Sometimes he wants
To play this game.
Then he wants to play that game.
But he doesn't really like either one.

Do you have days
When everything seems wrong?
Sometimes, do you complain
All day long?

When you see that you are complaining
About everything,
It could be that what you need
Is a good rest.

Take some time out.
Lie down for a few minutes
And you may become
A lot happier.
If that doesn't work,
Just say to yourself,
"I will not complain anymore."

"My bed shall comfort me, my couch shall ease my complaint."(Job 7:13, KJV)

Today I Feel Like God Is Close

How far away does God live?
Is He in the heavens?
Does He stay behind the moon?
Or does He live
On the other side of the world?

God lives in all these places.
And He lives very close
To you!

No one else is like God.
Only God can live every place
At the same time.

Every day and every night,
God stays beside you.

God never leaves you.
He always knows
What is happening
In your life.

Some days you feel like
God is close to you.
Other days you feel like
God is far away.

No matter how you feel about God,
He is always beside you.
God never goes away.

If you reach out your hand,
You can't feel God.
If you look all around,
You can't see God.

But He is always there,
No matter how you *feel*.

Say hello to God.

"But there is a friend who sticks closer than a brother."(Prov. 18:24, TLB)

Today I Feel Confused

June was listening to the radio
When she heard something strange.

Quickly she ran into the living room
To tell her parents.
"There is a tomato coming!"
She shouted.

The radio announcer had said,
"A tornado..."
And she thought he said,
"A tomato...."

It is easy to be confused.
We hear words
We don't understand.
We see people do things
Which we have never seen before.

We have so many questions
We would like to ask.
Why do we close our eyes
When we pray?
Why do mothers wear shoes
With high heels?
Why can't we see God?
Why do dogs walk on four legs?
Where does your father go
When he leaves for work?
Why do babies cry so much?
Why do people go to war?

We hear some things on television.
We hear other things
That we have never heard before.

It is easy to become confused.

It helps to ask questions.
Parents and teachers can help you.
Ask them the questions
Which make you confused.

When Jesus was young
He liked to ask a lot of questions.

**"Both hearing them, and asking them
questions."(Luke 2:46, KJV)**

Today I Feel Good

Some days you feel good
About yourself.
You picked up your toys,
Straightened up your room,
And washed your hands—
Without being asked.

You do so many things well.
You try to say thank you and please,
And sometimes you ask your parents
If you can help them.

That's great!
Sometimes you do things
That are bad.
But most of the time
You try to be good.

Your parents are proud of you.
You can be happy with yourself.

But don't forget to thank God
For all the good things
You can do,
And ask God to help you
Stay away from the bad things.

"Beloved, follow not that which is evil, but that which is good. He that doeth good is of God."(3 John 11, KJV)

Today I Feel Like Talking Mean

Does this ever happen to you?
Do you ever feel like
Telling everyone what to do?

When you are playing
With one or two friends,
Do you ever get "bossy"
And talk roughly to them?

Sometimes we get that way.
We want everyone
To play the way we say.
If he doesn't,
We might talk mean.

Wayne did that once.
His friend wouldn't
Play the way he wanted,
So he talked mean to his friend,
Took his ball and went home.

That wasn't nice.
The next time Wayne wants to play
With his friend,
He might say no.

It is so much better
If we remember to talk kindly.
People enjoy being around us more
When we talk nicely.

"Kind words are like honey — enjoyable and healthful."(Prov. 16:24, TLB)

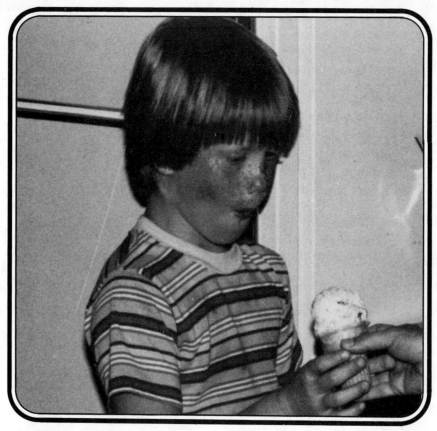

Today I Feel Thankful

There was once a boy
Who would break his toys.
If he stepped on them,
He didn't care.

He would push his toys off his bed.
If they broke, he just pushed them
Under the bed.

He never seemed to like what he had.
He always seemed to wish
He had what other people had.

This boy never said "Thank you."
He didn't like anything.
People didn't like to give him presents.
He would complain
No matter what he got.

There was another boy
Who enjoyed saying "Thank you."
He liked everything.
People wanted to give him presents.
Even if it was a piece of candy
Or a shiny apple,
His eyes would open wide.
And he would smile big.
Everyone knew he was going to say "Thank you."

He thanked parents, friends, relatives,
Brothers, sisters, neighbors,
Grandparents, and company.
When he prayed he liked to thank God.

He was happy for everything he got.
He didn't act spoiled or fussy.
He was glad to get things.
And he said so.

God says it is good to be thankful.
It makes us happy people.
Can you think of something
You are thankful for?

**"No matter what happens, always be
thankful, for this is God's will for you who
belong to Christ Jesus." (1 Thess. 5:18, TLB)**

Today I Feel Like Crying

I saw a grown man cry.
He was a baseball player.
His team had just lost
The championship game.

He was young, strong and talented.
But he couldn't keep the tears back.
It was all right for him to cry.

I watched a woman cry.
She was very happy.
She had just heard from the doctor
That her son would be healthy.

She was brave and smart.
It was all right for her to cry.

It is all right for you to cry.
No matter how old you are.
No matter if you are a boy
Or a girl.

Jesus Christ used to cry.
He didn't feel ashamed
To have tears
Rolling down His cheeks.

How do you feel when you start to cry?
Does your throat feel stiff?
Do your lips sometimes shake?
Do you try to hold the tears back?

That's how most of us feel.
Even if we try hard
The tears still come sometimes.

This is much different
Than pretending to cry.
Maybe you have done that, too.

Suppose you wanted some candy
But mother said, "Not now."
Instead of waiting,
You made yourself cry.

You didn't have to cry.
You just wanted to get your way.
Most of us grow out of
Pretend crying.

Everyone knows we are getting bigger
When we give up pretend crying.

When you have go cry,
It's all right.
God made us so that
We can cry when we need to.

**"A time to cry,
A time to laugh."** (Eccles. 3:4, TLB)

Today I Feel Like Helping

When you help your mother or father,
How does that make you feel?

When you carry dishes to the kitchen
Or take clothes to the washer,
How does that make you feel?

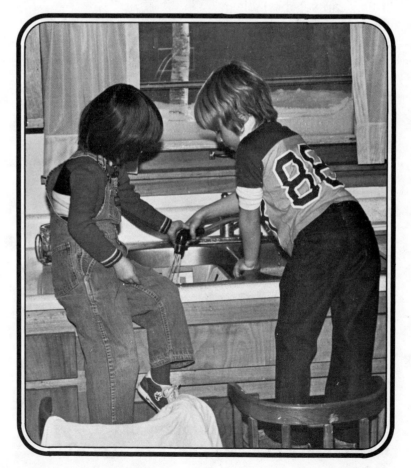

Have you ever
Straightened up your bed
Without being told to?
How did that make you feel?

It feels good
To be a helper!

It really feels good
To think ahead and to plan
How you can help.

Then you ask your mother
If you can set the table
Or help your brother
Pick up his toys.

When you help people,
Look at their faces.
Do you see them smile?
Do they say "Thank you"?
Do they pat you on the back
Or give you a big hug?

People are happy
When someone helps them,
And it makes you feel good, too.

God likes to see us help others.
God also likes to help us.
Helping people
Makes everyone feel good.

"I lie awake at night thinking of you — of how much you have helped me."(Ps. 63:6, TLB)

Today I Feel Ugly

Janis was sitting on her porch,
And she felt terrible.

Her dress was only three weeks old,
And she had torn it.

Janis' hands were dirty
And she had mud on her face.
Her hair was flying in every direction.

All of that was bad enough,
But something else happened.
Her best friend, Lisa,
Had gotten mad at her
And gone home.

Janis wanted to cry.
She felt dirty and alone
And ugly.
She just wanted to cry.

She felt awful.
But Janis wasn't really ugly.
She just *felt* that way.

Janis was still
The nice little girl
She always was.

Jesus Christ teaches us
That beauty is on the inside.
We can get dirty
And get scratches.
We can fall down
And get bruises.

We can do all of that
And still not be ugly.
Because beauty
Is inside your heart.

Love people.
Be kind.
Follow Jesus Christ.
Try to be like Him.

And you will always be beautiful,
Even with mud on your face.

"Create in me a new, clean heart, O God, filled with clean thoughts and right desires."(Ps. 51:10, TLB)

Today I Feel Embarrassed

Have you ever dropped
A dish of food on the floor?
Did your face turn red
When everyone looked at you?

You felt embarrassed.

Have you ever said something backwards
Or said a word in a funny way?
Did people laugh at you?

You felt embarrassed.

Sometimes we can feel
Our face turn red.
We wish we could hide behind a chair
Or pull our shirt up over our head.

We feel embarrassed.

Have you ever had
An adult tease you
About your hair
Or your clothes
Or your toys?

You felt embarrassed.

God made us that way,
So it must be okay.
After we're embarrassed for a while,
The feeling goes away.

"O God, in mercy bless us; let your face beam with joy as you look down at us."(Ps. 67:1, TLB)

Today I Feel Like Hiding

Jimmy had come home from school,
But no one knew where he was.
His mother looked in his bedroom
And his father looked in the garage.

But Jimmy wasn't anywhere.

His parents weren't worried,
But they were puzzled.
They called out his name.
Where could Jimmy have gone?

When his mother rang the bell for dinner,
Jimmy finally came.
He had been in a corner of the basement
Playing with his cars.

Why didn't Jimmy come
When his parents called?
Because Jimmy had been hiding.

When he came home from school,
Jimmy had been throwing stones in the yard,
And a stone hit the window and cracked it.

He knew he had been wrong to throw them
Near the house,
So he hid.
Jimmy was afraid to face his parents.

All of us feel like hiding sometimes.
Maybe your father
Forgot to get you a birthday present,
Or your sister broke your favorite doll.

It makes you want to hide
Because you feel hurt.

If you hide because
You feel guilty
You wonder what will happen
When you do come out.

Will people be angry with you?
Will you get a spanking?
Will you be sent to bed?
Or will everything be all right?

It is better to find out
Right away.
Tell the person what you have done.
Tell them you are sorry it happened
And really mean it.

Maybe you will be punished
And maybe you won't.
But it feels so good
To have it over with.
That feels better than hiding.

It feels great to be close
To the people
Who really love you.
And if someone who loves you
Has accidentally hurt you
Please tell that person about it.

**"He will carry the lambs in his arms and
gently lead the ewes with young."(Isa. 40:11,
TLB)**

49

Today I Feel Forgetful

Dennis couldn't find his sneakers anywhere.
They weren't in the closet
Where they were supposed to be.
They weren't behind the door.
He even looked
In his toy box.
He couldn't find his sneakers anywhere.

Dennis couldn't remember
Where he had put them,
And it was time
For him to leave for school.

Suddenly he remembered.
He had left them
Outside the back door
Because they were muddy!
It's easy to forget.

But sometimes you forget
Because you don't want to remember.
Your mother told you
To pick up your toys,
But you forgot
Because you didn't do it
Right away.

Once in a while
We pretend to forget.

But many times we really do forget.
And we didn't want to forget.
Then we feel sorry.

All of us forget sometimes
And it's all right.
But we try hard to remember.

God doesn't have that problem.
He never forgets.
God knows who you are—
Today, tomorrow and forever.

Thank you, God,
For remembering my name.

"Yet God does not forget a single one of them."(Luke 12:6, TLB)

Today I Feel Like Hugging

Do you like to be held?
Do you ever feel the need
To have someone's arms
Wrapped snugly around you?

Most of us like to be hugged.
Strong, busy fathers enjoy it.
Loving, caring mothers need it.
Kind, patient grandparents can hardly wait.

A schoolteacher described a "bear hug"
To her students this way:
A bear hug is a big strong hug,
Not just a little one.

After she described it,
All the students went home
And gave "bear hugs"
To their parents.

It made all the children
Feel great.
It made the parents
Feel wonderful, too.
Everyone was happy
And felt loved.

What is a hug?
A hug says, "I like you."
A hug says, "You are all right."
A hug says, "You are special."

When someone hugs me,
I know he cares about me.
It makes me feel good about myself.

That is why it is important
To give hugs.
Your parents, brothers, sisters and friends
Need hugs, too.

Jesus met a man
Who was sick.
No one ever touched the man.

Jesus reached out
And touched him.
He wasn't sick anymore.
It made both of them
Feel good.

Hug someone today.

"Jesus reached out and touched the man."(Luke 5:13, TLB)

Today I Feel Like Getting Even

When was the last time
A person did something
To hurt you?

Maybe he broke your dump truck,
Or called you a name,
Or even hit you.

What did you do then?
Did you want to hit him back?
Did you want to call him a name
Or break something of his?

Children aren't the only ones
Who like to get even.
Adults can be the same way.

But getting even always hurts someone.
Jesus doesn't like that.
He teaches us to be kind
Even when someone
Is mean to us.
That doesn't sound easy.
We want to hurt the person
Who hurts us.

Jesus Christ said we should be kind
To people who are kind to us
And also to people who hurt us.

Next time someone
Knocks your bike over,
Remember,
Jesus doesn't want you
To knock *his* bike over.

If everyone did what Jesus taught us,
Soon we would stop hurting each other.

"There is a saying, 'Love your friends and hate your enemies.' But I say: Love your enemies." (Matt. 5:43, 44, TLB)

Today I Feel Important

Ann Marie was going out.
She put on a clean dress
And was ready when her father
Got his coat.

Her father took Ann Marie
To a little restaurant
And bought her a glass of pop.

For a long time
They sat,
Drank,
And talked.

They talked about anything
Ann Marie wanted to talk about,
And Ann Marie knew
She was important.

The word important means special.
Ann is very special to her father.
No doubt about it,
Ann Marie is important.

When do you feel special
Or important?
Is it when someone holds you
And reads to you?

Do you feel important when
Your mother or father
Plays ball with you?

Do you feel special when
Someone gets new clothing
For you?

It feels good
To feel important.

You are important
To the people around you.

They are parents, grandparents,
Uncles, aunts, brothers, sisters,
Teachers, friends, and God.

Maybe you are special to one person.
Maybe you are special to many.
But you are special or important
To someone.

Doesn't that feel great?

Listen to what Jesus Christ said about you:

"Not one sparrow (What do they cost? Two for a penny?) can fall to the ground without your Father knowing it. And the very hairs of your head are all numbered. So don't worry! You are more valuable to him than many sparrows."(Matt. 10:29-31, TLB)

Today I Feel Grouchy

Do you ever have a day
When nothing seems to go right?
Your food isn't good.
Your clothes don't fit.
Your brother doesn't
Treat you right.

Maybe, for no good reason,
You just feel grouchy.
If anyone gets near you,
You might "bark" at him.

We can stop being grouchy
If we want to.

Listen to yourself.
Do you sound hard
To get along with?
Then tell yourself
You will be as nice
As you can be
The rest of the day.

It feels good
To *stop* being grouchy.

"Think about things that are pure and lovely, and dwell on the fine, good things in others." (Phil. 4:8, TLB)

Today I Feel Lazy

Some days you don't feel like doing anything.
Maybe you stayed up too late last night.
Maybe you didn't eat right today.
Maybe you even have a cold
And you don't feel very well.

All of us feel lazy sometimes.
We want to lie around
And not do much at all.

Once in a while, you shouldn't do anything
But rest until you feel better.
But most of the time
You should just say "No" to laziness.

Tell it to go away!
Your room still has to be straightened up.
Your clothes still need to be folded
And your toys are still on the floor.

If you let laziness win too often,
You could become a lazy person.

When it is time to get the job done,
Stand up, straight and tall,
And go to work.

You can rest later,
When the job is done.

**"A lazy fellow has trouble all through life;
the good man's path is easy!"(Prov. 15:19,
TLB)**

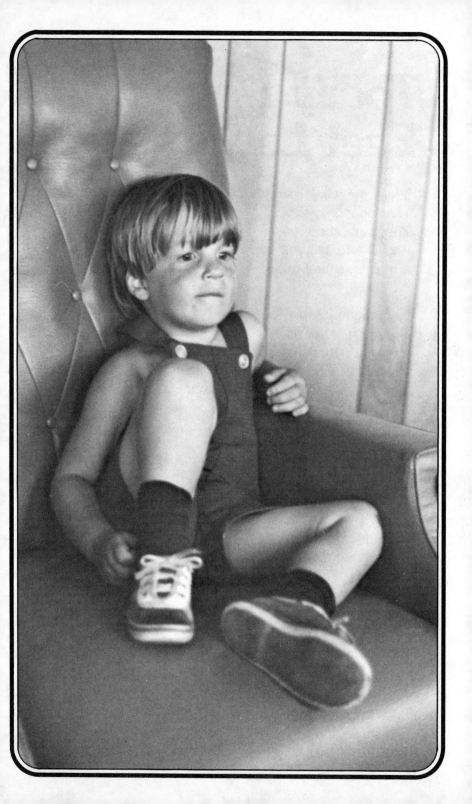

Today I Feel Loved

It feels great to know
That people love you.
They care about you
And like to see you happy.
It makes us feel good
All over.

How many people love you?
Do you have parents
Or grandparents,
Or do you have brothers and sisters?
Maybe you have a good neighbor
Or a special friend,
Or maybe a schoolteacher.

There are so many people
Who love us,
And we often forget
Who they are.

How do you know
If someone loves you?
Some say, "I love you."
Others just give you a good,
Tight hug.
A few people give presents
Or write letters.
Some just like to have you around.

Brothers and sisters
Love each other.
But some don't
Like to say so.

If you could look inside,
You would find
They love each other, too.

It feels especially good to know
That Jesus Christ loves us.
Every day, no matter what happens,
The Son of God keeps on
Loving you.

**"I have loved you even as the Father has
loved me."**(John 15:9, TLB)

Today I Feel Guilty

Bill's dad asked him
If he wanted to play ping-pong,
But Bill didn't want to.

That seemed strange.
Usually Bill begged
To play ping-pong.

So his dad asked him again.
But not tonight.
Bill's dad didn't know it
But Bill didn't want to
Go *near* the basement.

Earlier in the day,
Bill was throwing a ball
In the basement
And he broke a flower pot.

Bill knew he wasn't supposed to
Throw a ball in the basement.
Now he felt guilty
And was afraid his father
Would notice the broken pot.

It isn't any fun to feel guilty.
You know you did something wrong,
And now you are afraid
Someone will find out.

You have to be careful
What you say.
You have to be careful
Where you go.
Sometimes you have to be careful
Who sees you.

Inside you feel terrible,
Because you know
You did something wrong.

All of us do something wrong sometimes.
And when we try to hide it,
We only make it worse.

God has a good way
To make us feel better
When we feel guilty.

We can tell our parents
What we have done
And tell them we are sorry.
Sometimes we will be punished
And sometimes we won't.
But we will feel better
Right away!

Let's ask God to help us
Do it the *right* way next time!

"I confess my sins; I am sorry for what I have done."(Ps. 38:18, TLB)

Today I Feel Like Loving

Mark is a young boy
Who has a brown dog
With one large, black spot
And long ears that hang down.

Mark plays with his dog every day.
Mark loves his dog.
He calls him Brownie.

It feels nice to love
A special pet.
It feels good to hold it
Or to have it snuggle in close.

We love our parents.
We care what happens to them.
It is good to have parents around.
When they are away we think about them.
We love them and it feels good.

Many children have grandparents
And they love them
Even if they are far away.

Children love their brothers and sisters,
But they don't always say so.

It feels good to love God.
We know He loves us,
And it feels great to love Him, too.

"We love him, because he first loved us."(1 John 4:19, KJV)

Today I Feel Picked On

It happens once in a while.
Two of your friends get together
And they tease you.

Maybe they make fun of your clothes
Or they laugh at the way you run.
Maybe someone you don't even know
Calls you a nasty name.

What is going on?
You are being picked on.

It doesn't happen every day,
But when it does
It makes you feel very bad.

You feel like calling them names
Or laughing at the way they talk.
But that won't help.
They will probably just
Pick on you more.
And Jesus said that we should
Love our enemies.

This happens to everyone sometimes,
And it hurts.
But if you forgive
And treat them kindly anyway,
Tomorrow you will be friends again,
And you will forget all about it.

It isn't any fun to be picked on.
The next time you feel like
Picking on someone,
Remember that.
Then you won't tease other people,
Because you know it hurts
To be picked on.

If you don't pick on other people,
Other people might behave better, too.
Jesus Christ told us
To treat each other kindly
As we ourselves want to be treated.

"Go easy on others; then they will do the same for you."(Luke 6:37, TLB)

Today I Feel Like Being Polite

Do you like to make people feel good?
It's fun to see other people
Smile and look happy.

You can help them
By being polite.

Being polite
Isn't hard.

All you need to remember
Is to say and do
Nice things for others.

That doesn't
Sound hard.

When you ask for something,
Remember to say,
"Please."

When you get something,
Remember to say,
"Thank you."

When you want to do something,
Remember to say,
"May I?"

That doesn't
Sound hard.
Maybe you say those things already.

If you do,
You are a polite person.
The words you use
Can make people happy.

Make someone happy today.
Say something polite.

"When she speaks,
Her words are wise,
And kindness is the rule
For everything she says."(Prov. 31:26, TLB)

Today I Feel Useless

Andrew is five years old.
He is growing up,
But some days he feels bad
About being a child.

He thinks,
"I wish I were a grown-up.
Then I could do things."
Andrew feels useless.

But one night,
Andrew's family
Locked themselves
Out of their house.

Andrew's father and mother
Tried to open every window
But they couldn't.

Finally, they opened
A tiny window.
But Andrew's father couldn't fit
Through the window.
Andrew's mother couldn't fit either.
Andrew said, "I can fit."
Father lifted Andrew up
And he climbed through
The tiny window.

In just a minute
Andrew was through the house
And opening the door.

Andrew isn't useless.
Every child is a person.
Every child is valuable
To other people
And to God.

You are a valuable person.
Jesus Christ loves children
Just like you.
He knows a child is a person.
You are a person.

**"Beware that you don't look down upon a
single one of these little children."**(Matt.
18:10, TLB)

Today I Feel Like Praying

Praying may sometimes be hard,
But it doesn't have to be.
Praying can also be
Just like talking to a friend.

Sometimes children are afraid to pray.
Adults are often afraid to pray, too.

They think they have to use long words,
Or use a deep voice,
Or say something special.

If praying is that difficult,
They think maybe
They had better not try.

Praying is really easy—
Like talking to your brother,
Sister, mother, father, or neighbor.

Do you have something
You would like to say to God?

Would you like to thank Him
For something special?
Would you like to ask God
To do something or help you?
Maybe you want God to help a friend,
Or you just enjoy telling God
How you feel.

How would you talk to a nice person
Or a friend?
That is the same way
You can talk to God.

Prayer is talking.
It is talking to someone who cares.

Tell God what is on your mind.
And tell Him in simple words
Like you use every day.
God would enjoy hearing from you.

"How I thank God for you, Timothy. I pray for you every day." (2 Tim. 1:3, TLB)

Today I Feel Hurt

Bryan is a good boy,
But sometimes he forgets.
One day he rode his bike
Over Mr. Anderson's grass.

Mr. Anderson came running out
And stopped Bryan.
Mr. Anderson was angry.
He yelled at Bryan
And told him never to
Ride on his grass again!
Or—Mr. Anderson would call
Bryan's parents.

Bryan felt bad
As he rode his bike
Slowly home.
He felt hurt inside.

Have you ever been yelled at
By someone who was angry?
That's no fun
Even if you did do something wrong.

How do you feel
When you hurt inside?
You don't feel like smiling.
If someone wants
To play a game,
You probably won't want to.
Sometimes you don't even
Want to eat.

Being hurt feels even worse
If you didn't do
Anything wrong.

The bad feeling
Will go away.
You will start
To feel better again.

The smile
Will come back.
We hurt,
But only
For a little while.

You will be happy again,
And probably soon.

"A cheerful heart does good like medicine, but a broken spirit makes one sick."(Prov. 17:22, TLB)

Today I Feel Worried

Once in a while
A child worries about something,
And no one knows about it.

He might worry about a big dog
Down the street.
But the child doesn't want
To tell his parents.

There was a child
Who had to cross a wide,
Busy street.
That street worried the child,
But he didn't want
To tell his parents.

Some nights he stayed awake
Worrying about that street.

Many times we worry about something
For just a little while
And then we forget about it.
But sometimes we worry day after day.

One of the best ways
To get rid of a worry
Is to tell someone
About it.

We can explain it to a friend,
Or tell it to our parents,
Or talk to a teacher
Or someone else we like.

Often our worry goes away
Just because we talked about it.
At other times someone can tell us
What to do about our worry.

Do you ever worry about
Your parents,
Your grandparents,
Fires,
Getting lost,
Or being hurt?

When you do worry,
It feels good
To talk to someone.
It might be a big help.

Be sure to tell God
About your worries.
You can talk to Him
Anytime and anywhere.
He would like to hear
About the things
That worry you.

"Let him have all your worries and cares, for he is always thinking about you and watching everything that concerns you." (1 Pet. 5:7, TLB)

Today I Feel Like Pretending

Do you ever put on a funny hat,
Or wear your father's shoes
Or your mother's make-up?

It's fun to pretend.

Do you ever pretend to be
A clown,
Or a teacher,
Or an astronaut,
Or a minister?

It's fun to pretend.

Do you ever hide under the covers
And play cowboys,
Or mountain climbers,
Or sailors?

It's fun to pretend.

It's fun to be a child.

"When I was a child, I spake as a child, I understood as a child, I thought as a child."(1 Cor. 13:11, KJV)

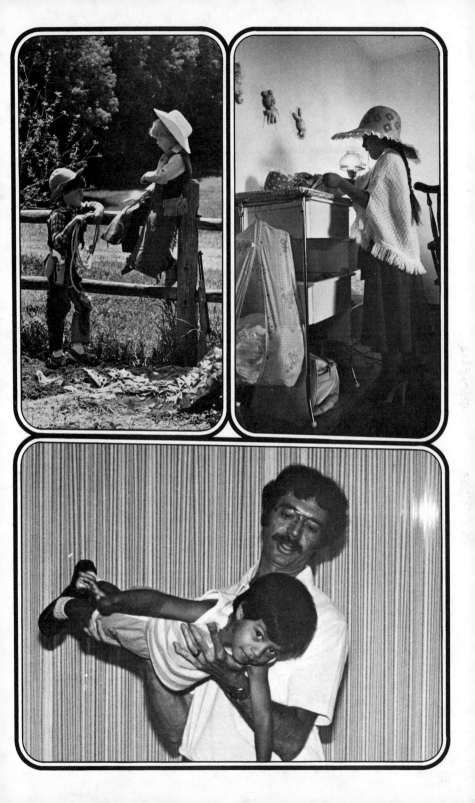

Today I Feel Jealous

Mary got a brand new coat,
But Lori still had an old coat.
Lori felt bad about her coat
Because she was jealous.

It is easy to become jealous
If we let ourselves.
We look around at what
Other people have
And we wish we had it.

Allen got a new television set.
Joan has two bikes.
Robert has racing cars.
Pam got a new dress.

We feel badly
When we don't have
What our friends have.
This is jealousy.

Children aren't the only ones
Who get jealous.
Adults sometimes feel the same way.

Jealousy hurts us
Because it makes us forget
All the good things we have.
Then we don't want to
Thank God
For all He has given us.
Instead we complain
About what we don't have.

Would you like a happy heart?
You can begin by thinking
About how good God is to you.

Do you have food?
Do you have clothing?
Do you have a home?
Do you have someone to love you?

You don't need to be jealous.
God has been good to you.

Name three things or people
You are happy to have.

Hasn't God been good to you?

"For jealousy and selfishness are not God's kind of wisdom." (James 3:15, TLB)

Today I Feel
Like Being Quiet

It's fun to make noise.
You like to sing, talk, shout,
Ring bells, play radios, and pop balloons.

It's fun to laugh out loud,
Tell stories, or maybe whistle.
If we couldn't talk
Or make a sound,
We wouldn't like that.

But sometimes we enjoy
Being another way.
It can also be fun
To sit still
And just be quiet.

We turn off all the sounds
And listen to the quiet.

You might like to read
Or look at magazines,
Or see Bible pictures,
Or color,
Or daydream,
Or think about God.

Quiet can be beautiful.
Quiet can be peaceful.
Quiet can feel good.

"Be still, and know that I am God." (Ps. 46:10, KJV)

Today I Feel Left Out

All of Jim's friends were invited
To Paul's birthday party.
But somehow Paul forgot
To invite Jim.

That really hurt Jim's feelings.
He didn't like being left out.
None of us do.

We like to know people care
And think about us.
We like to know
Someone wants us around.

But all of us get left out
Sometimes.
Two of your friends are playing together
And don't have time for you.

That doesn't mean
They don't like you.
They just got busy
And forgot to include you.

None of us can be included
All of the time.
Some days we will get
Left out.

That's all right.
Put on a big smile.
Find something else to do,
Or find another friend.
Tomorrow you can be
Back together again.

None of us
Are completely left out.
Every day
And every hour
God stays close to us.

We are never alone.
We always have someone
Who cares,
Because God treats us
The same way
Every day.

Thank you, God,
For never leaving us out.

"For God treats everyone the same." (Rom. 2:11, TLB)

Today I Feel Little

It is hard to be a child
When everyone around you
Is so big.

Parents are tall.
Chairs are big.
Bookshelves are high,
And car seats
Are too low for you
To see out the windows.

Some days you wish
You were big enough
To reach the candy
On the top shelf
Without climbing.

It's all right to be little.
No one knows for sure
How tall you will be
When you grow up.

If you are tall
Or if you are short,
It isn't important.
What really counts
Is what kind of person
You are.
Nice people come in little sizes
And big sizes.

God told Samuel to go
And pick out a king.
Samuel selected a tall,
Handsome man for the king.

God told Samuel, "No,
I want David.
The short one
With the rough skin."

If you are little,
It is all right with God.
He loves you
Just the way you are.

**"But the Lord said to Samuel, 'Don't judge
a man's face or height.' "(1 Sam. 16:7, TLB)**

Today I Feel Lonely

On most days
There is someone around
To play with.

But on other days
You are all alone.

It might be raining
And no one
Wants to come over.

But maybe
Other people
Are just as lonely
As you are!

They wish they had
Someone
To play with.

You wish you had
Someone
To play with.

But both of you
Sit home
Alone.

If you don't want to be alone,
Why not call your friend
And ask him to come over?
You could have a good time
Together.

Lots of people
Get lonely.
And they are waiting
For someone
To call them.

Do it!
Give that person
A call.

**"A man that hath friends must shew
himself friendly."**(Prov. 18:24, KJV)

Today I Feel Like Sharing

Can you remember
When someone was eating an orange
And suddenly he reached over
And handed you a piece?

You probably smiled,
Said "Thank you,"
And thought how nice
That person was.

We knew a man
Who always carried
Candy, nuts or gum
In his pocket.

He would always give
Some to our children.
Our children smiled,
Said "Thank you"
And thought how nice
This man was.

You know how to share.
You have given your toys
To a friend to play with.

You have probably given
Half an apple,
Some of your pop,
Or extra clothing to a friend.

It's fun to share.
Everyone feels better.
And the more we share
The easier it becomes.

In Kansas City
The policemen share.
They give children
Pictures of football players
And pieces of bubble gum.

Children and policemen
Become better friends
Because they share.

If we share our things often
It becomes easier to share.
When we become adults
We will keep on sharing.

Sharing is important to God.
He decided to share His only Son.
God sent Jesus Christ to earth
To share His love with us.

It is good to share.
God is pleased,
And it makes people happy, too,
When you give some
Of what you have.

**"For God so loved the world that he gave
his only begotten Son."(John 3:16, KJV)**

Today I Feel Like Lying

Do you ever feel
Like you have to tell a lie?
Most people feel that way sometimes.

Maybe you spilled some milk
And you wanted to blame it on the cat.
Maybe you took a toy from your sister
And you said you didn't.

At first it sounds easy.
You could tell a lie
And maybe get away with it.

But you would know
You had lied.
And sooner or later
Your parents might find out
You lied.

Naturally God knows
If you lie.
And someday your friends
Will find out you tell lies.
Lying could get you
Into a great deal of trouble.

Even though we may feel like lying,
It is better to tell the truth.
We will do less harm
By being honest.

Then we won't hurt
Our parents,
Our friends,

God,
Or ourselves.

It is good
To have friends
That you can trust
All the time.

You know
They wouldn't
Lie to you.

It is great
To be
That kind of friend.

That's the way
God wants you to be.

"Don't tell lies to each other."(Col. 3:9, TLB)

Today I Feel Like Shouting

I like to make noise.
It's fun to laugh,
Or yell at a football game,
Or sing
At the top of my voice.

Imagine if there were no noise
And everyone had to whisper
All the time.
We wouldn't like that.

Noise is good
When it is used
At the right time
And in the right place.

We should never make noise
When we are told to be quiet.
We should not make noise
If it is bedtime.
We shouldn't make noise
When someone else is talking.

But at the right time
And in the right place
It's fun to shout.

"Let them shout with delight, 'Great is the Lord who enjoys helping his child!' " (Ps. 35:27, TLB)

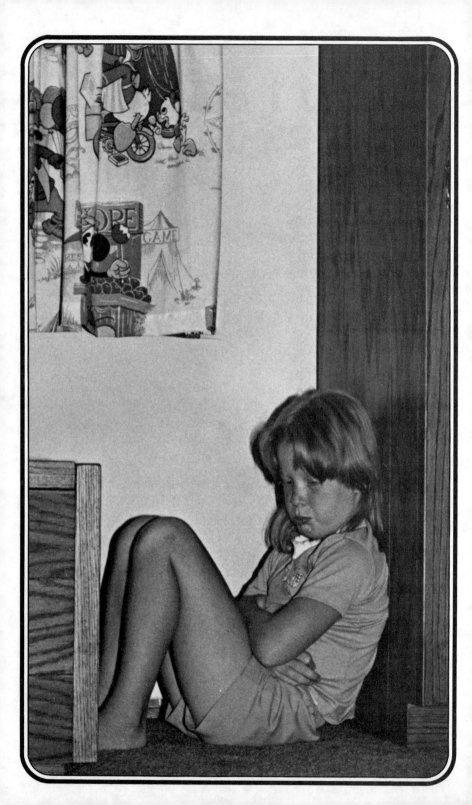

Today I Feel Like Pouting

It's fun to get what you want.
You enjoy playing your favorite game
Or going to your favorite park.
You want to get the dessert
You like best.

We are all this way.
There are some things
We like
And we are happy
When we get them.

You are just like
Everyone else.

But what happens
If you don't get
What you want?

Sometimes we just sit
And pout.
There are so many ways
To pout.

Some of us won't talk to anyone
When we are pouting.
Some people hang their head
And look as sad as they can.
Other people won't share
When they are pouting.

Some act mean
And almost bark
When they say something.

None of us are pretty—
When we pout.

Pouting says:
"I wanted my way
And I didn't get it.
Now I am going to act nasty."

Adults can pout, too.
But they try
To keep from pouting.

Many times you try
To keep from pouting,
Don't you?

Sometimes you don't
Get your way
And you say,
"That's all right."
You don't always
Have to have your way,
Do you?

Today you *feel* like pouting,
But you decide to be happy instead.
You don't have to have your own way.

We don't have to be
Like King Ahab.
When couldn't get
The land he wanted,
The King went to his room
And pouted.

**"So Ahab went back to the palace angry
and sullen. He refused to eat and went to
bed with his face to the wall."(2 Kings 21:4,
TLB)**

Today I Feel Tired

There are so many things to do.
There are friends to play with,
And bikes to ride,
And exciting games to try.

On most days
You can find something to do
From early morning
Till late at night.

God has made
Such an interesting world.
There are so many places to hide,
So many things to see
That we have never seen before—
Like green bugs that wiggle funny.

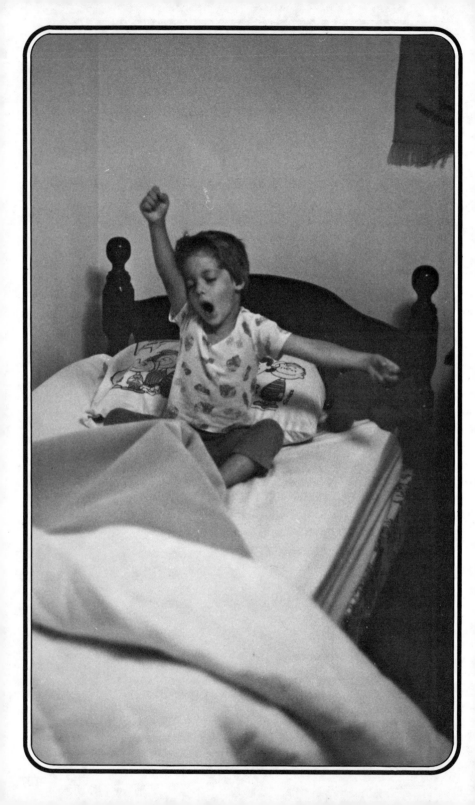

After you do things for hours and hours
Your body starts to slow down.
Often your eyes begin to look tired
And partly closed.

When you start to feel this way,
It's time to give your body a rest,
Even if you don't want to rest.

God made your body
To do many things.
But when it gets tired,
You need to take care of it.
Maybe you need a nap
Or even a good night's sleep.

But that's all right.
If you rest now,
You can do so many
More things
When you wake up.

Rest is God's plan
For keeping your body healthy.
Jesus had many things to do every day.
But sometimes He had to rest
Just like you do.

"Then Jesus suggested, 'Let's get away from the crowds for a while and rest.' For so many people were coming and going that they scarcely had time to eat."(Mark 6:31, TLB)

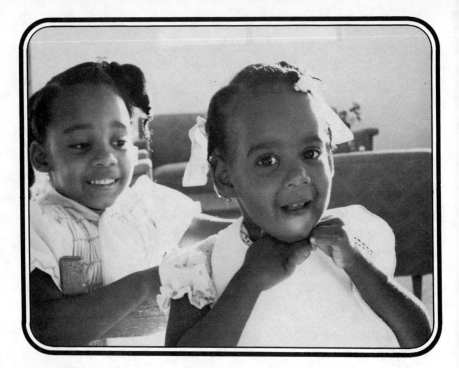

Today I Feel Like Singing

There is music all around us.
We hear it on television,
On the radio, on tapes,
And on records.

We hear music in stores,
And in churches,
And in schools,
And in our homes.

Most people like music
And enjoy singing.
Some sing with others.
Some sing by themselves,

And others sing only
If they are all alone
And no one can hear them.

Some families like to sing
Before they eat.
They sing a "thank you"
To God
For their food.

Singing is fun
For so many reasons.
When you are happy
You can say so
By singing.

When you want to praise God,
You can do it in songs.
When you want to have fun
With your friends,
You can sing together.

Some children
Even make up
Their own songs
And sing them.

There are so many
Interesting things to do.
Singing is one
Of the happy
Things to do.

"Sing a new song to the Lord." (Ps. 96:1, TLB)

Today I Feel Sad

When do you feel sad?
Did you ever have a favorite toy
Break into pieces?
Did you ever have a pet die?

There are many things
That can make you sad.
Both children and adults
Become sad, sometimes.

It's all right to feel this way.
Even God must feel sad sometimes—
Especially when He sees us
Treat each other unkindly.

Just remember that the sadness
Will go away.
Soon you will smile again
And be happy.

Sadness is a part of life
And it hurts for a while.
It may take time,
But the sadness will go away.

"I will be glad, yes, filled with joy because of you."(Ps. 9:2, TLB)

Today I Feel Sorry

Janet's mother had told her
To put the milk away.
But Janet was busy
Playing with a friend.

Janet forgot
To put the milk away,
And the next day
The milk was spoiled.

Janet's mother
Had to throw
The milk out.

When Janet heard
About the milk,
She felt very bad.

She liked to please
Her mother.
But Janet knew
That this time
She had not.

Janet felt so sorry
She wanted to cry.
She went to her room
And sat alone for a while.

What should she do?
How could Janet show
Her mother how sorry
She really was?

Staying in her room alone
Helped for a little while.
It gave her time to think.
But Janet decided not to stay there
Too long.

Janet went to her mother
And said,
"I'm sorry about the milk.
Next time I'll do it
Right away"

Her mother was so happy.
She wrapped her arms around
Janet
And hugged
And hugged
And hugged.

Everything was all right now.
And the next time
Her mother told her
To do something,
Janet did it right away.

"I am sorry for what I have done."(Ps. 38:18, TLB)

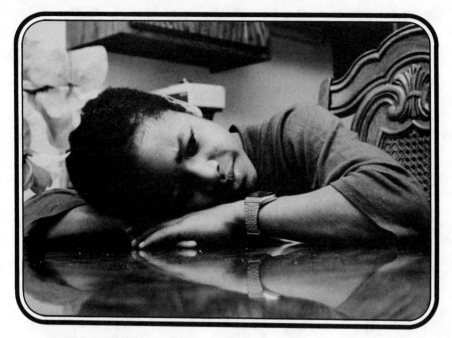

Today I Feel Like Staying Up Late

Do you hate to go to bed sometimes?
Most children like to stay up.
If they could, many would go to sleep
On the floor, still watching television.

That is one of the reasons why we need parents.
They know more about healthy bodies
And clear minds than children do.

Parents know that if children don't get enough sleep,
Their bodies become tired and worn down.
Then it is easier for children to get sick.

When people don't get enough sleep,
They sometimes become grouchy
And they have a bad day.

Some children need to sleep a long time.
Others don't need as much sleep.
Parents help by deciding how much they need.

There are different ways to behave at bedtime.
Some always complain about going to bed.
A few disobey and get into trouble.
But many children know they need sleep.
They go when it's bedtime
Without fussing.

Even if you want to stay up late,
It is usually better if you get lots of sleep.
And while you are sleeping,
God will watch over you
And care for you.

"Then I lay down and slept in peace and woke up safely, for the Lord was watching over me."(Ps. 3:5, TLB)

Today I
Feel Sick

Our bodies are strong
And can fight off
Most sicknesses.

Germs try to get in,
But your body
Won't let them.

But once in a while
Sickness takes over,

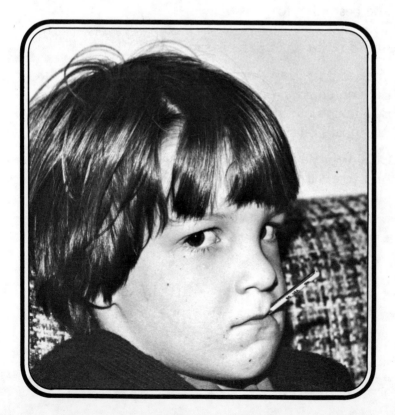

And your body
Starts to feel it.

Maybe your nose will run
Or you will begin to cough.
Maybe your body will get warm
And your head will feel hot.

Sometimes your head begins to hurt
And you have to go to bed
And sleep for a while.

When you are sick
You feel badly
And don't want to do
Anything.

When you feel sick,
The best thing to do is
To relax
And do what your parents say.

You want to feel better soon,
But you could get more sick
By running around
And going outside.

Obey your parents
And you will be well
Much faster.

"Children, obey your parents."(Eph. 6:1, KJV)

Today I Feel Like Talking

There is a little girl
Who comes home from school
Ready to talk.

Lisa has done so much
During the day.
She has worked, colored and played.
Now she wants to tell someone
All about it.

Usually her mother stops to listen.
But other times, her mother is busy.
Lisa will have to wait.
That's hard.
Lisa wants to talk right now.

When her mother finishes her job,
She sits down
And Lisa tells her all about her day.

It's fun to have someone
To talk to.
You have just made a toy house,
Or climbed a tree,
Or found a golden button.
Often you run quickly
Just to tell someone about it.

At other times
You have questions to ask.
How can a worm see under the ground?
Do horses sleep standing up?
Does God have a wife?

Usually when you want to talk,
You are probably like Lisa:
You want to talk right now.

If you have to wait sometimes,
It's all right.
Your mother, father or friend still loves you.
They still care about what you do.
Later, when they get their job done,
They will sit and listen.
Then you will be able to share
Everything you can hardly wait to tell.

Sometimes, when you are waiting
For someone to listen,
Why not talk to God?
He is interested in hearing
About everything you do.

"I love the Lord because he hears my prayers and answers them. Because he bends down and listens, I will pray as long as I breathe!"(Ps. 116:1, 2, TLB)

Today I Feel Like Being Stubborn

What does stubborn mean?
It means you won't
Change your mind
Even if you are wrong.

You have seen stubborn people.
Someone may say,
"You can't play with my cars."
He knows that is unkind,
But he still won't let you
Play with the cars.
He is being stubborn.

We are all stubborn
Once in a while.

Can you think
Of some times
When you
Have been stubborn?
You probably can.
We all
Have been stubborn.

It's no fun to be stubborn.
It isn't kind or caring.

Try this.
After you say,
"No, you can't,"
To a friend
Or a brother
Or a sister
And then you know
You could have said "Yes,"
Go ahead and say "Yes."
Don't be stubborn.

All of us could be kind.
It's nicer
Than being stubborn.

"Instead, be kind to each other."(Eph. 4:32, TLB)

Index of Feelings